When You Are HAPPY

By Eileen Spinelli

Illustrated by Geraldo Valério

Simon & Schuster Books for Young Readers
New York London Toronto Sydney

MY GRANDMOTHER

MY GRANDFATHER

MY MOM

MY BROTHER

SIMON & SCHUSTER BOOKS FOR YOUNG READERS

An imprint of Simon & Schuster Children's Publishing Division

1230 Avenue of the Americas, New York, New York 10020

Text copyright © 2006 by Eileen Spinelli

Illustrations copyright © 2006 by Geraldo Valério

SIMON & SCHUSTER BOOKS FOR YOUNG READERS is a trademark of Simon & Schuster, Inc.

Book design by Einav Aviram

The text for this book is set in Pink Martini.

The illustrations for this book are rendered in acrylic.

Manufactured in China

2 4 6 8 10 9 7 5 3

CIP data for this book is available from the Library of Congress.

ISBN-13: 978-0-689-86251-9

ISBN-10: 0-689-86251-2

MY GRANDMOTHER

MY GRANDFATHER

MY DAD

MY SISTER

To Jer, who finds me when I'm lost.

And to our children and their partners,
who show up on the doorstep whenever I am lonely.

And to our grandchildren,
who make me dizzy with joy.—E. S.

À minha mãe, Zeca—G. V.

When you are sad,
I will hold you.
I will let you cry.

I will catch your tears
in a blue cup
and water the yellow flowers
and they will grow
more beautiful.

When you are cold,
I will weave you
a blanket
from leftover sun.

I will sing summery songs
for you until
my voice cracks,
and I will watch you
warmly
until I become
the firelight
dancing in your eyes.

When you are sick,
I will sit by your bed
quietly waiting
in case you
should want something—
warm soup, chamomile tea,
painted rainbows,
poems piled like pillows
around your head.

When you are lonely,
I will show up
on your doorstep
with my heart in
a basket.
I will whisper
"I love you"
until your loneliness
grows wings
and flies off
like a silken bird.

When you are afraid,
I will take your hand
and not let go—
except once
to borrow
one hundred tiny stars
to spell out the words:

They will shine above you
forever,
even in the darkest dark.